VIKING

Published by the Penguin Group
Penguin Group (Australia)
707 Collins Street, Melbourne, Victoria 3008, Australia
(a division of Pearson Australia Group Pty Ltd)
Penguin Group (USA) Inc.
375 Hudson Street, New York, New York 10014, USA
Penguin Group (Canada)
90 Eglinton Avenue East, Suite 700, Toronto, Canada ON M4P 2Y3
(a division of Pearson Penguin Canada Inc.)
Penguin Books Ltd
80 Strand, London WC2R 0RL England
Penguin Ireland
25 St Stephen's Green, Dublin 2, Ireland
(a division of Penguin Books Ltd)
Penguin Books India Pvt Ltd
11 Community Centre, Panchsheel Park, New Delhi – 110 017, India
Penguin Group (NZ)
67 Apollo Drive, Rosedale, Auckland 0632, New Zealand
(a division of Pearson New Zealand Ltd)
Penguin Books (South Africa) (Pty) Ltd
24 Sturdee Avenue, Rosebank, Johannesburg 2196, South Africa

Penguin Books Ltd, Registered Offices: 80 Strand, London, WC2R 0RL, England

First published by Penguin Group (Australia), 2012

1 3 5 7 9 10 8 6 4 2

Text and illustrations copyright © Fiona Roberton 2012.

The moral right of the author/illustrator has been asserted.

Cover design by Kirby Armstrong, Penguin Group (Australia)
Text design by Kirby Armstrong, Penguin Group (Australia)
Typeset in 22/31 pt Archer Book
Colour separation by Splitting Image Colour Studio, Clayton, Victoria
Printed and bound in China by South China Printing Company

National Library of Australia
Cataloguing-in-Publication data:

Roberton, Fiona.
Cuckoo / Fiona Roberton.
978 0 670 07612 3
Cuckoos—Juvenile fiction.

A823.4

Fiona Roberton

Cuckoo!

zzz

PENGUIN|VIKING

WIBBLE   WOBBLE

Cuckoo hatched,

POK!

and all was well.

Until the other birds discovered Cuckoo...

...was different.

They couldn't understand a word Cuckoo was saying.

No matter how hard Cuckoo tried.

It was all extremely confusing for everyone.

So Cuckoo decided it would be best
if he left, and bravely went in search of
someone who *could* understand him.

He spotted some sheep in the distance
and flew over to say hello.

But the Sheep couldn't understand him either,

and neither could the Frogs.

Or the Pigs.

Or the Snakes.

Or the Cows.

Or even the Rabbits.

CAACKAA!

THUMP!

THUMP!

THUMP!

pat
pat
pat

Cuckoo just couldn't seem to find anyone
who spoke his language.

But then Cuckoo had a brilliant idea.
He would learn theirs instead!

But even though Cuckoo tried...

and tried...

Sssssssock!

THUMP!

THUMP!

THUMP!

pat

pat

pat

as hard as he possibly could, he just
couldn't get the hang of any of them.

CUMONKSSSSSS
BAGRITUUCKOO
THUBIITOOOMP!

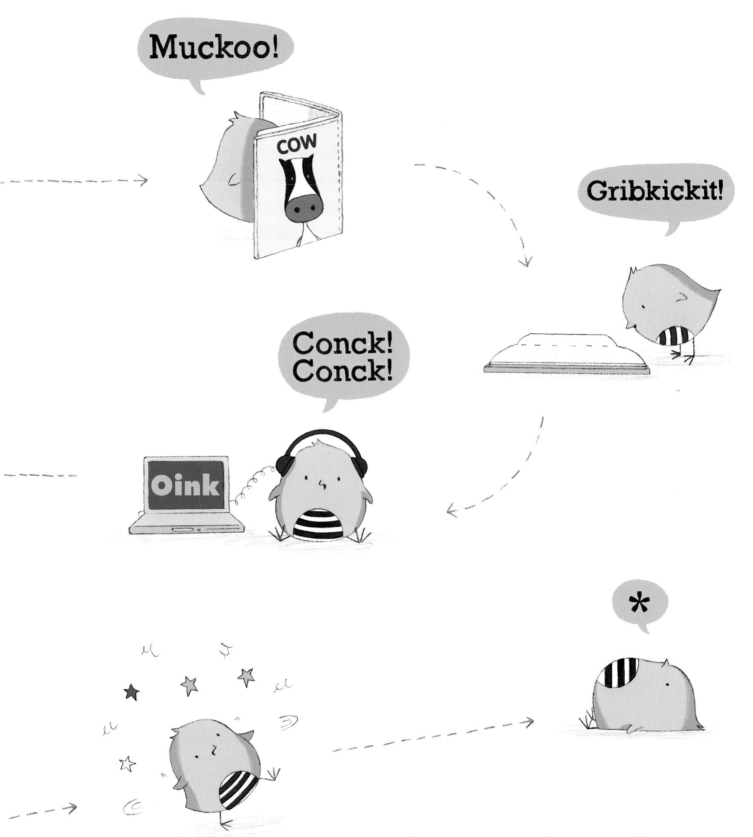

Cuckoo was exhausted.
His brain hurt from all the learning.

He flew up into the rooftops to find a nice warm spot to sleep, and was just about to close his eyes…

...when from out of the twilight,
he thought he heard the faintest...

Cuckoo!

Cuckoo couldn't believe his ears.
It couldn't be...could it?

Cuckoo raced as fast as his little wings could carry him, from window...

to window...

to window, till at last...

...he finally found...

Cuckoo!

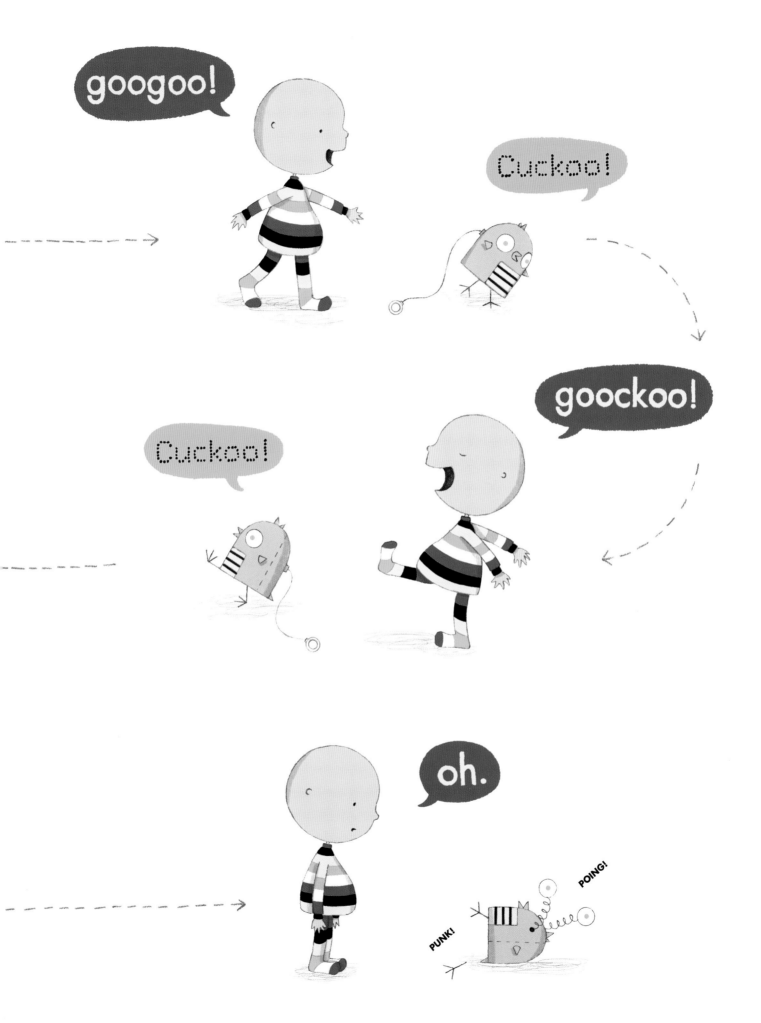

cuckoo?

Cuckoo!

Someone who understood him…

…perfectly.